The TURNING of the YEAR

BILL MARTIN JR

ILLUSTRATED BY GREG SHED

HARCOURT BRACE & COMPANY

San Diego New York London

Library of Congress Cataloging-in-Publication Data
Martin, Bill, 1916–
The turning of the year/Bill Martin, Jr.; [illustrated by] Greg Shed.
p.   cm.
Summary: Describes the characteristics of each month
in rhyming text and illustrations.
ISBN 0-15-201085-8
[1. Months—Fiction.   2. Stories in rhyme.]   I. Shed, Greg, ill.   II. Title.
PZ7.M3643Tu   1998
[E]—dc21   96-53078
First edition
A C E F D B

Printed in Singapore

The illustrations in this book were done in designer gouache on canvas.
The display type was set in Goudy Village Italic.
The text type was set in Kennerley.
Color separations were made by United Graphic Pte. Ltd., Singapore.
Printed and bound by Tien Wah Press, Singapore
This book was printed on totally chlorine-free Nymolla Matte Art paper.
Production supervised by Stanley Redfern and Pascha Gerlinger
Designed by Kaelin Chappell

For Danielle and Rudy
—B. M.

For Chanel and Trent
—G. S.

In January, out I go

to welcome winter's icy blow.

In February, bound with snow,

I sled the hillside, top to toe.

In March,
the warming noontime sun
spells the end
to winter's run.

In April, springtime sets me free
to splash through puddles recklessly.

In May, strong branches dare me be
a squirrel in the apple tree.

In June,
the warm earth fashions green
and insects sing
good-bye to spring.

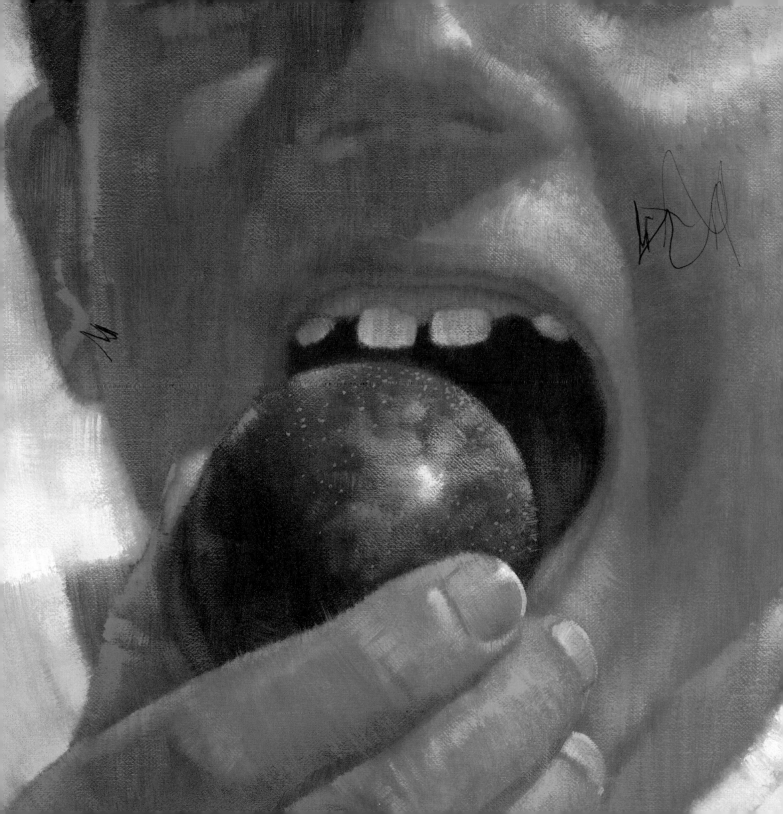

In July, summer calls me come
to taste the ripening wild plum.

In August, on hot days I run
through harvest fields that praise the sun.

In September,
summer calls its ending
with blue haze
and chrysanthemums blending.

In October, autumn calls me out
to see the maples' raucous shout.

In November, cool days lure me out
to gather pumpkins strewn about.

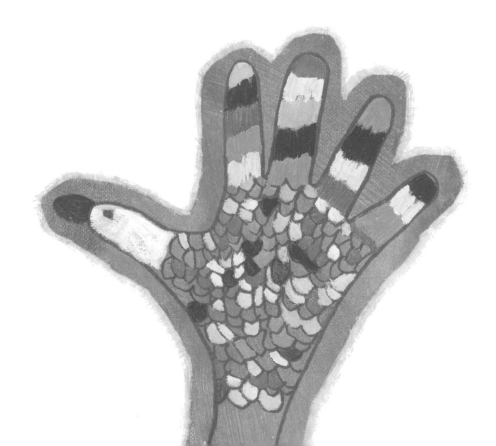

In December,
autumn calls its warning,
"Get ready
for a winter morning!"

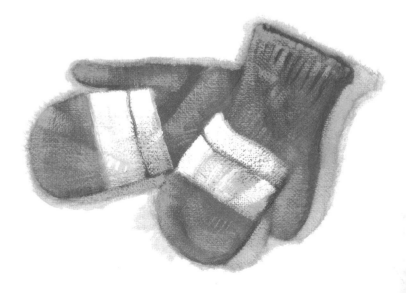

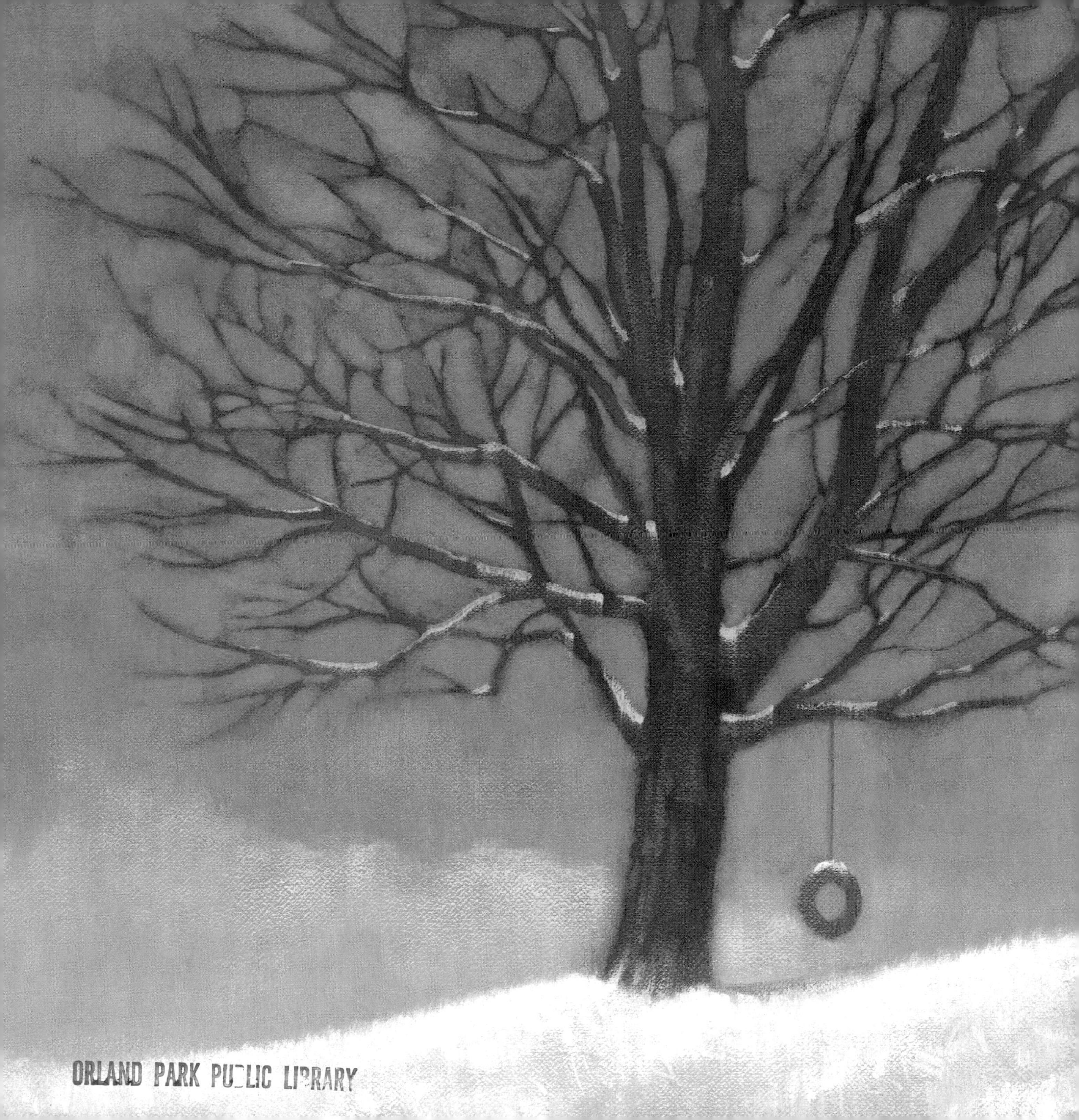